E.G. Rand

# TOMBSTONE TEETH AND OTHER HORRORS

ISBN 978-1-09836-207-2 eBook 978-1-09836-208-9

# TOMBSTONE TEETH

Tombstone Teeth, Tombstone Teeth,
Buried under, six feet deep
Cover your eyes, turn your head
If he sees you, you'll be Dead.

S carborough was like many old New England towns. Scarborough had history, it had families, it had secrets. One of those secrets was the haunted cemetery. That patch of earth had a curse that predated the town settlers. The local tribes had warned the colonizers not to build there. That it was a hunting place, stalked by a spiritual predator. But the settlers figured any place was safe for a house of God, so they built it anyway. Before the church was finished a worker was decapitated by a falling beam and his blood mixed into the foundation of the building. When it rained, blood would seep down the steps of the church. It happened for a decade after the workman's death.

Two years after the church was built there was more blood spilled, this time during an autumn Sunday mass. The priest was just beginning the fire and brimstone when it suddenly became dark as night. The building groaned like a ship on turbulent seas. As if crushed by pressure, one of the prized glass windows shattered inward. It peppered a pew of townsfolk with glass and it killed four year old Sarah Stevenson. A shard pierced her throat. Witnesses claimed thunderous laughter resounded in the church as the child bled to death.

That was when some people named the presence in the church-yard. The children began to call it Tombstone Teeth. They sang its song during recess and whenever they had to walk by the churchyards iron gate. The song was an incantation to keep the monster at bay. None of them wanted to be locked up forever with Tombstone Teeth like poor little Sarah Steveson. Some said that on a full moon, Sarah could be seen crying for her mother from the gate of the cemetery.

The town began to fear their church. The bells rang at night for no reason at all. People heard giggling, saw moving shadows. Even the priest, who viewed himself as a direct representative of God, felt uncomfortable in that dark narthex. Some townsfolk said when they passed the churchyard they heard laughter, others heard sobs. Always emanating from the ceme-tery, something moving among the tombstones. Tombstone Teeth, looking for its next victim.

The church mysteriously burned down during a snowy winter in 1776. They knew that one of their own had done it, but they were more relieved than upset. The mill was being built and the town was growing by the day. They built a new church in the heart of town, and abandoned the wreckage of the old chapel to the woods.

There was still the problem of the cemetery. The villagers didn't know what to do with the old churchyard as they respected the dead as much as they feared that horrible place. So they put up a great stone wall around the cemetery and they topped the wall with shards of shattered glass. Then they locked the wrought iron gate, and considered the matter done. But the dark sexton of the cemetery did not abide by gates and locks, and it was still hungry.

---

In 1886 Scarborough was booming. A new mill turned a high profit and provided plenty of work. Its owner, a prominent industrialist named William Christensen Eglinton, was a generous man. He bought a new roof for the church in town and always made sure his workers were cared for. While in Scarborough he married nineteen year old socialite, Lily Farming.

William decided to build a country mansion for his young bride. He bought land near the cursed cemetery, now a great wilderness the locals called "Church Park." Everyone tried to dissuade him, but William would not turn down a good deal based on rumor, suspicions, and a few old boxes of bones. Besides, Lily was an avid spiritualist. William was sure nothing would make her happier than ghosts to commune with.

The mansion he built was lavish. They employed many servants from town, and imported wall paper and furniture from all over the world. The mansion was just as beautiful as Lily, and just as susceptible. The Elingtons quickly became the height of the town's social elite. They hosted elaborate dinner parties with flowing champagne and fine china. Anyone who was anyone was invited. Lily continued to dabble in spiritualism, and hosted her spiritualism group in a special seance room designed by her.

But she did not have to look far to find things to speak with.

She reached out, and the darkness of the cemetery found her. The night began to whisper to Lily. It called her out of the house, told her horrible things, showed her horrible things. She grew wan, spent more and more time in the woods. Once the servant girl, Molly, followed Lily during one of these woodland walks. Molly claimed that Lily walked a well worn path through the forest to the old cemetery. There Lily stood before the rusted gate, eyes wide and blank, whispering into the weeds and tombstones and giggling at whatever spoke back.

Then came the evening of October fifth.

Lily had planned a midnight seance. She added allure by making it exclusive, inviting only two of the wealthiest couples in town, The Fitzpatricks and the Joneses. She persuaded her husband to join. Lily was excited-- she told them she had found a spiritual teacher who would lead them to something amazing.

At a quarter to midnight, Molly brought in a tray of tea. The room was lit with candles, illuminating the polished circular table. Lily looked paler than usual in a green velvet gown. The night was cold and fire crackled in the fireplace behind her. To her left was her husband, smiling indulgently. The guests were laughing and joking, ready for an evening of fun. A chair had been left intentionally empty for Lily's spiritual guide. Molly put down the tray and left.

At one a.m. Molly and the cook, Bailey, were in the kitchen and heard an odd noise. An unmistakable laugh, deep and nasty, resonating in the house. A tinkling of shattered glass, then a long moment of silence, followed by a cacophony of screams. Bailey and Molly rushed to the top of the steps but the door was locked. Bailey ran back down to get the master key in the kitchen while Molly attempted to kick down the door.

Bailey got the key, fitted it, but when the door swung open the screaming stopped. They were all floating... Mr Elglinton, the Joneses, and FitzPatricks. They floated in slow circles, hanging above the table as if strung up by invisible rope. Their eyes bulged, their mouths gaped like hooked fish.

Then, before Bailey and Molly's eyes, they dropped. Mr Eglington and his guests died on the seance table, bulging sightless eyes looking at Molly in the doorway. All of the windows in the room were shattered inward. Lily was nowhere to be found.

Pete Furn, the grounds keeper, was the last person to see Lily Eglinton alive. He lived in a cabin at the edge of the forest, so when he heard the commotion he came out with a torch. He saw Lily in a blood soaked green gown. He called out to her but she didn't respond. She was too far away. Pete Furn claimed she was floating. He tried to chase her, but she disappeared into the thick forest. The last thing he heard was her fading voice in the wind, some old nursery rhyme-- "Tombstone Teeth, Tombstone Teeth, buried under six feet deep--"

---

Patrick Smith got out of the office early on Friday and arrived at his country farmhouse just as the snow began to fall. He settled in to get some peace and quiet. It was Jeanine's night to take Stella to gymnastics. Three nights a week was a lot, but Stella showed an aptitude for it and was making friends. However, sitting through a two hour practice after the office was a long day and Patrick was looking forward to some time to himself. He lit a cheery fire in the farmhouse grate and poured himself a beer. He was watching the snow fall when a car pulled up and shattered his reverie.

It was an ancient Toyota, held together by duct tape and will. It limped into the driveway, spewing exhaust into the cold air. Patrick's good mood curdled as his sister-in-law got out of the car. She was completely covered in a ridiculous neon pink coat, but he didn't have to see her face to know it was Terri. Patrick wrenched open the front door before she could knock.

She looked worse. The decline had been steady the past couple years, and now she was skeletal. Terri was a ghost of the beautiful girl she used to be. Her face was a shriveled apple, covered in lurid sores. Her expression was surprised. She had likely hoped to get her sister home alone. The disappointment was obvious.

"I need to talk to Janine," Terri grumbled. No greeting, no hello to the family member that she hadn't seen in weeks.

"Not here," Patrick sneered. The beater Toyota steamed in the driveway. Patrick hoped that meant Terri would leave. It was snowing harder now, and behind Patrick the fire crackled.

"I really need to talk to her--"

"Yeah, well, she's really not here," Patrick interrupted. Terri didn't even ask about her own daughter. Not that he was surprised, Terri rarely showed up for her scheduled visits with Stella, and Stella had stopped asking about her mom. After an awkward silence Terri cut to the chase.

"Jeanine said I could stay here for a couple nights."

Patrick let out a humorless laugh. There it was, the real reason Terri was here. Patrick went to shut the door in her face

"You can't leave me out here Patrick! It's snowing! I don't have anywhere else to go!"

There was always a disaster with Terri, always some big problem. When was everyone going to learn that the "big problem" was just her? Patrick continued closing the door, almost locked--

"You can't do this Patrick, I am family! You-YOU STOLE MY DAUGHTER! YOU BASTARD!"

Patrick was generally a patient man, but this he could not abide by. Again he wrenched the door open, startling his sister-in-law back across the porch.

"STOLE YOUR DAUGHTER?" Patrick screamed, red-faced, "STOLE?!"

Terri fumbled back, but missed the step and fell hard in the snow. Patrick strode to the end of the deck and stood over her, hissing through clenched teeth.

"I did not steal your kid. You dumped her on us, just like you dump shit on anyone who has ever known you. You are no family of mine, you are not staying in my house, and you are not getting another dime from me unless it's to get your tubes tied."

Terri had never been spoken to like that before. She was dumb-founded, sprawled on the lawn. Patrick's breath was ragged. His outburst surprised himself. He turned away from Terri, now strangely deflated. He said over his shoulder,

"Go on, Terri. Get the fuck off my lawn."

Patrick shut the door to his warm little farmhouse and locked it.

———

Diego did not know Terri well. She sometimes hung around the bar where he worked, usually with a male friend. She had been looking worse lately, looking sicker. That evening she had come up to the bar and asked for a ride to her sister's house because it was snowing. Diego was raised to believe that when someone needed help, you helped them.

But he had not signed up for this. As Terri slunk moodily back into the car, Diego began to panic. Giving this girl a ride home was one thing, but he had his own problems to deal with and wasn't in the market for more. They sat in tense quiet, Terri's face hidden in her enormous coat. She was crying.

"So… do you have… somewhere else?" Diego felt awkward. Terri snuffled into a handful of bloody tissues, then coughed something unintelligible.

"What?"

"I said, take me to the junction of Old Mill Road and Landenberg. I'll walk from there."

Diego took her. It was snowing hard now, and he felt a pang of guilt as she got out of the car. There was nothing out here, just Church Park, the ruins of the old mansion and cornfields. But before Diego could stop her Terri had strode into the trees, towards the cemetery. Diego drove home in silence, clouded by a sense of dread.

Terri had walked this path before. This wasn't the first time she had been turned away from her sister's house. At least that guy giving her a ride saved her the walk to Church Park. She would cut across, going around the old cemetery wall, to the other side of town. From there she could get to Orchard Trailer Park. She knew a few dealers there, maybe one of them would let her crash and she could score a fix.

Terri hugged herself, shivering violently. It was so cold. She needed a hit, she didn't have any money, and her asshole brother-in-law turned her out onto the street. Now she's got to blow some dealer for dope and a dirty mattress on the floor. If only it had been Jeanine who had answered the door. Then she'd have some cash, maybe a clean bed. Jeanine was always there for her, but then she went and married that asshole. Now Terri was welcome nowhere, and a stranger to her own daughter.

Tears blurred her vision as she picked through the forest. It was quiet here. She walked along the old stone wall around the cemetery, six feet high with jagged glass stabbed into the top, quickly being hidden beneath the snow. When Terri was younger she had wondered about the broken glass. Why would an old churchyard need so much protection? The old mansion didn't have any broken glass, not that it needed any. Anything of value was long gone. These days the mansion was just bones and fallen beams, a shell of its past beauty. Just like Terri.

At the top of the hill Terri stopped, leaning against the wall and breathing heavily. She was so weak, and it was so cold. Her body shuddered and heaved like an old car, she couldn't remember the last time she had eaten or slept for more than an hour.

A noise hissed behind Terri, a familiar sound. The squeaking of an open gate.

Terri may have been dope sick, but she knew that there was only one gate in and out of the old cemetery. The only gate was the wrought iron one in the front that was always locked.

And yet here she was, looking at an open gate into the cemetery. The land was dark, overgrown, and caked with snow. Tombstones poked out from the brush. Mausoleums loomed like monoliths. Light flickered just inside the gate.

There was a small fire in the cemetery. A "hobo" fire, Terri used to call them before she herself was an addict. The fire crackled happily in a tin garbage can. Next to it was a little lean-to, dry from the snow. It even had a blanket inside.

She was so cold, and so sick. It looked like someone had made themselves a nice little camp and then been called away somewhere. Maybe they had sisters who didn't marry assholes. But still, where had the gate come from?

She was lost in thought and didn't realize she had walked through the open gate. The fire was warm and comforting. Terri figured that whoever set up camp must've decided they didn't need it after all and left. She settled into the tent and realized that what she had thought was a blanket was actually an old piece of green velvet. Terri held it up, a green velvet and lace dress. It was old and musty, crusted with a large copper stain.

There was a creak and a slam. Terri leapt to her feet. The gate had closed. And not only was it closed, the gate was gone. Where she had come in was now only a stone wall.

There was a sudden gust of cold air, and the fire went out like a candle. Terri didn't realize how dark it was until the fire was gone. The snow muffled the sound, but she heard something, a whisper in the wind.

"Don't… my… dress…"

Terri tried to run but couldn't. Her feet were in the earth up to her ankles, as if the ground was consuming her.

The snow in front of her pulsed once, twice, then burst like an infected sore. Out rose a corpse, a skeleton barely held in place by rotting flesh, a few long blonde hairs clinging to its scalp. It turned to face Terri, eyes long gone but still seeing. A smokey darkness swirled, grotesquely puppeting the body. The corpse's jaw dropped open and a scream filled the air.

"DON'T TOUCH MY DRESS!"

Terri screamed. The ground buckled. The skeleton swooped towards her, then was tossed aside like a discarded doll. Its bones clattered across the cemetery. Now it was just the smokey darkness, which had rolling eyes and jagged teeth. It consumed Terri, filling her lungs and eyes, choking her. Tombstone Teeth pulled the life out of Terri as it laughed a horrible laugh.

---

Jeanine sat in the gymnastics center watching Stella. Stella was not the most graceful of the girls, but she was the most determined. Doggedly doing backflip after backflip until she could land it.

Jeanine checked her phone again. It had been a week since she had last heard from Terri. Terri had never gone this long without checking in. And she wasn't in the hospital or jail, Jeanine regularly checked both. She usually met up with her sister about once a week. They would get a coffee, and Jeanine would slip Terri some money. Jeanine neglected to inform her husband Patrick about these visits. She knew what he would say; he'd call her an enabler and he would be right. But Patrick didn't know. He didn't know what it was like to love an addict the way Jeanine loved her sister.

Patrick had been behaving strangely too, come to think of it. A few days ago Jeanine asked him if Terri had called or dropped by, and he immediately got defensive. He accused her of not trusting him, going so far as to storm out of the room. He spent the rest of the evening in his office playing video games. The next day he pretended nothing had happened.

Jeanine wasn't a suspicious woman, and it wasn't like Patrick's feelings about Terri were unknown to her. In fact, Terri was the only thing they truly disagreed on. She wanted to chalk his outburst up to exhaustion. He had been working so much lately. Still, she suspected there was something he wasn't telling her.

As she stared at her phone it started ringing. An unknown number. In excitement she answered, hoping it was Terri.

"Mrs. Smith? This is Lieutenant Wess from the Scarborough Police Department."

Jeanine's heart popped like a balloon. She left the gym to take the call. She didn't want Stella to see her face.

Lieutenant Wess asked Jeanine if she had seen Terri in the past week. A friend of hers, Diego, had called in worried about her.

"He had given her a ride to the corner of Old Saw Mill and Landenberg and hadn't seen or heard from her since. I figured I would call you and ask if you or Patrick had seen her since they got into that argument..."

"Argument?"

"Yes. Apparently Diego drove Terri to your house. He said that when Terri got there, she and Patrick had a big fight and he turned her away. I take it he did not tell you about this?"

Jeanine's stomach twisted. She was vaguely aware of the gymnastics practice wrapping up behind her. She had to hold it together for Stella, but how was she going to deal with Patrick lying to her face? She was so lost in thought she didn't hear the Lieutenant speaking.

"Ma'am? So you haven't seen your sister?"

"No. No, I haven't heard from her either. She must be in trouble-- we have to look for her officer, something terrible must have happened--"

Infuriatingly, the officer chuckled.

"She probably went somewhere to cool off, stayed with a friend for a while."

"So you aren't going to look for her?" Jeanine felt like her throat was closing up. Terri was well known down at the station, and was arrested again last September for prostitution. Every time the police caught her they treated her worse. To them, Terri wasn't human. Just bothersome garbage.

The officer assured Jeanine that if Terri didn't show up within the next week or two they would do a missing persons report, and then he hung up. She went back inside to Stella, who was on cloud nine. She had finally landed the perfect backflip, and insisted on showing Auntie Jeanine several iterations of the trick. Stella had bonded with Jeanine, but never called her mom or mommy-- a nomenclature she saved for Terri. Jeanine listened to Stella's happy chatter on the way home, and found herself stifling tears.

Once they arrived at the farmhouse Stella zoomed in to regale Patrick with the stories of her perfect backflip. Jeanine walked into the kitchen and poured herself a glass of red wine. She listened to Patrick and Stella laugh, Patrick asking her if she had math homework she needed help with. Despite his many resentments towards Terri, Patrick never took it out on Stella. He loved her as if she was his own child. It was one of the many things Jeanine loved about him. Her hands shook as she drank the glass and poured herself another.

Eventually Stella thumped off to her room, closing the door. Patrick came into the kitchen, smiling broadly.

"Hey babe! Where is my hug? You don't even--"

He saw her face and stopped.

"Why didn't you tell me you had seen Terri? That she came here?"

Patrick sighed. He knew his interaction with Terri would come back to haunt him, they always did. He sat down at the table and stared at his wife. Outside the bone cold moon was high, casting a square of bluish light on the floor of the hallway.

"She's missing, Patrick. She's missing and you were one of the last people who saw her. How could you not tell me? She could be in trouble--"

"Oh for God's sake she's ALWAYS in trouble Jeanine!" Patrick snapped. "Okay, yes, she showed up here. She asked if she could stay here and I said no-- which, if I recall, you and I had agreed upon."

Jeanine bit her lip. Patrick was right. When Jeanine and Patrick first took in Stella, Terri had been allowed to spend the night during her visits. But when Patrick's heirloom watch turned up in the pawn shop, Patrick had laid down the law. He said that either Terri was banned from the house, or Jeanine could go sleep on the street right next to her. Jeanine, angry at Terri herself, agreed to uphold the banishment.

"You should have told me you saw her. You lied to me." Jeanine turned towards Patrick. Great tears rolled down her face, streaking her makeup. The wind went out of Patrick's anger and he got up to hold his wife. Outside the cold wind howled, and for the first time Patrick considered that maybe something had happened to Terri.

They settled into a reluctant truce, going about the rest of the evening as normal. But Jeanine didn't sleep in the marital bed that night. She told herself she wanted to be near the landline in case the cops called, but really she didn't want to sleep next to Patrick. She was angry with him for lying to her. This sleeping arrangement was fine with him; he was sick of the whole thing. Jeanine put Stella to bed and lit her nightlight. She was just shutting the door when Stella made an odd, strangled sound. As Jeanine watched, Terri's voice came from Stella's mouth.

"The gate is open!"

Stella was sitting up in bed, eyes open and unseeing. Her mouth hung ajar, not moving with the words. Her night light set a white cast on her face.

"The gate... is..."

Suddenly, Stella relaxed. She settled into her bed.

"What? What did you say?!" Jeanine found herself frantic. She knew Terri's voice had just come out of Stella's mouth. But, amazingly, Stella was already asleep.

And now Jeanine was alone on the couch. The night was bitter, wind rattled the window frames of the cottage and seeped under the front door. Jeanine walked to the front window and turned the porch lights on. Was hearing Terri's voice in Stella's room just her imagination? A fantasy brought on by her worries? But Jeanine couldn't shake the feeling that Terri was right outside the door, freezing and lost, looking for Jeanine to rescue her.

But as she looked out at her yard Jeanine saw nothing, just snow. Great piles of swirling snow. She pulled an armchair next to the fire and sighed. She had called the police station earlier to nag them, and they had reluctantly made a missing persons report. They also agreed to send some officers to ask around about Terri. At the time it had made Jeanine feel better.

Jeanine must have dozed off. She awoke minutes later to a familiar noise, the front door slamming. She leapt to her feet, hoping feverishly that it was Terri. But no one was there. Jeanine threw open the door and saw footsteps in the snow across the lawn, and the small figure of Stella retreating into the forest.

Jeanine got her boots and her jacket, tearing out after Stella. But she didn't think to grab a flashlight. Beyond the circle of the porch light the night was dark. The snow muffled sound and stung her face. Jeanine heard something on the wind, Stella's voice dreamily singing an old nursery rhyme.

"Tombstone Teeth, Tombstone Teeth..."

Jeanine gave chase. Her eyes adjusted to the dark and she followed a fumbling path of small footprints. How had Stella gotten so far ahead of her? It felt like miles, but Jeanine found herself at the junction of Old Mill Road and Landenberg, right near Church Park. This was the last place anyone had seen Terri. The cold stung, but Jeanine was sharp now. Stella's voice carried back to her on the wind.

"Buried under, six feet deep..."

Jeanine was familiar with this path. Back when she was young she and Terri crept around here, going to Orchard Park or drinking beer and smoking weed in the mansion ruins. Stella was ahead of her, but now Jeanine was closing the gap. She was going straight towards the old cemetery. Jeanine hoped Stella would stay on the path. She could see flashes of Stella's pink pj's between branches and snow.

Stella stopped short and Jeanine almost crashed into her. Jeanine grabbed her stiff body. Stella was ice cold and motionless, but she pointed to the wall of the cemetery.

"Buried under, six feet deep, cover your eyes, turn your head..."

"Stop it! Stella STOP IT!" Jeanine was hysterical. Stella's pajamas were soaked. She tugged but Stella wouldn't budge. She heard an unearthly giggle. It did not come from Stella. Jeanine followed Stella's point.

There was an illuminated archway in the fence. But this part of the cemetery had no entry. The only gate in or out was the wrought iron one in the front. The opening glowed strangely and inside the darkness of the cemetery something was moving. A sparkling blackness swirled, a blackness with a wide and toothy smile.

Jeanine grabbed Stella and wrenched as hard as she could. Stella, still cold and stiff, would not move. To Jeanine's horror Stella was somehow rooted in the ground. Stella stopped singing the nursery rhyme and began to scream for her mother:

"MOMMY! MOMMY! MOMMY!"

Something emerged from the cemetery. A large pink coat, filthy and covered in snow. Jeanine's stomach dropped. Wrapped in the coat was her sister's dead body, jerking towards them from the darkness. Terri's head lolled. Her face was bloated and green, her eyes shrunken in her skull.

Something was behind her, pulling the strings of a gruesome puppet. A great swirling blackness, a blackness with teeth. An ancient parasite using her sister's body as bait. Stella was no longer rooted in the earth. She tried to run to her mother. Jeanine struggled to hold her back.

"NO," screamed Jeanine. "YOU CAN'T HAVE STELLA!"

The creature jerked Terri's body. Her neck made a sickening crack and her head fell sideways at an angle. Tombstone Teeth grinned around her, a great mouth in the darkness. Stella was still screaming for her mother, twisting against Jeanine's grip.

For a second Jeanine had an insane thought to just let her go. Terri was finally gone, why not cut the last millstone and be free of it? Terri, the girl who had ruined her own life and tried to ruin Jeanine's in the process. Terri who never apologized, Terri who always wanted more. Terri who dumped a traumatized child on her doorstep and almost ended her marriage... Why not just let go?

But that wasn't her in her head. Tombstone Teeth had gotten to Jeanine. She fought him; she gripped Stella harder. Jeanine howled at the creature that took her sister.

"GO BACK TO HELL, TOMBSTONE TEETH!" Jeanine screamed.

There was a sudden vacuum of sound, the pop of oxygen filling a space. Jeanine stared at the cemetery wall, solid as ever. She still held onto Stella fiercely, but Stella no longer struggled in her grip. Stella was limp. Jeanine was dizzy. She could see something neon pink against the wall, but couldn't quite make it out. The sky swirled above her, and she was so cold. The last thing Jeanine saw before losing consciousness was Stella, sleeping peacefully in her arms.

<hr />

Officer Grady strolled through Church Park. Normally he would resent being sent out on such a bullshit errand as chasing after Terri. He was sure she was holed up with some boyfriend and was likely to turn up when she needed money. But Church Park was particularly radiant at dawn, and it had snowed the night before. The forest glittered in the early morning light. Enjoying the bucolic beauty, Officer Grady whistled as he strolled down the path to the old cemetery wall, expecting to find nothing but a hot cup of coffee at the diner later.

He was horrified when he found what appeared to be three dead bodies in the snow outside the wall of the old cemetery. He called for backup, leaning down to examine the corpses. One looked like it had been there for a while.

And that was how Officer Grady found the body of Terri, the woman he was so sure was alive moments ago. It looked like Terri had been dead several weeks. Her body was perched atop a pile of earth, as if the ground had thrown it up. As he finished phoning it in, Jeanine began to groan-- not dead after all.

At the hospital Jeanine and Stella were treated for mild frostbite. Jeanine more so because she had laid on Stella during the night and kept her warm. Stella remembered none of it--as far as she knew, she fell asleep in her bed and woke up in the hospital. Patrick was beside himself. He had woken up that morning to an empty house, the cars in the driveway. He called the police and tried to find tracks but it had snowed so much in the night that they were covered. At the hospital Patrick alternated between fiercely hugging his family, apologizing to Jeanine for lying to her, and weeping into his palms about all the horrible things that could have happened.

The hospital informed Patrick what Jeanine already knew. Terri was dead. The police were baffled. They had searched the path a few times and somehow missed Terri's body. The coroner ruled the death accidental; an autopsy showed that Terri had been dehydrated and emaciated at the time of her death. It appeared that she had walked into the woods, gotten disoriented and froze to death. The cops told Patrick this information in hopes that he could deliver it more gently to Jeanine. They also suggested that he not tell her about the large cuts and marks found on Terri's body. The coroner said they were probably caused by scavenging animals, but he was lying. No animals in the area had claws like that.

Patrick stroked Jeanine's hand as he told her of Terri's death. The doctors had said there was no way they could have saved her. The strain on her body was just too great.

Patrick would help finance a beautiful funeral for Terri, and together they would explain it to Stella in the simplest terms that they could. Mommy had gone into the woods and had an accident. They agreed to not ask how Stella had known where her mother's body had been, or why she had looked for her that night. Some things were better left unasked.

"She was called to the open gate," Jeanine muttered. Outside a cold wind blew, rattling the windowpane. Patrick looked at her quizzically, but just then Stella bounded into the room. The night in the hospital hadn't dampened her spirit. She threw herself onto Jeanine, and the three of them hugged each other. For a moment, the memory of the night's horror melted away.

Scarborough rested under its blanket of snow. Or rather, it waited. Because something still lurked in the cemetery, something hungrier than ever lay in wait behind the tall stone wall. It would only be a matter of time before a susceptible person happened by. But until then Tombstone Teeth watched, and waited.

# A BAD HANGOVER

There are few things worse in this world than waking up with a hangover. I don't mean a mild headache. I'm talking about a real mean bitch of a hangover, the kind that makes you feel like roadkill and fills your soul with a sense of dread. That's the kind of hangover I woke up with.

First sensations: the cold of the floor on my face and the pungent smell of vomit. Best case scenario, I collapsed on the floor next to my bed. Opening my eyes is painful. I blink into focus like an old camera-- I am not in my bed. I am not even in my house. I am in a darkened room somewhere, near a covered window because I can hear the early morning chirp of the birds. The singing is comforting.

I lift my body with great effort. I feel poisoned. Well technically I am poisoned. Still counts if you do it to yourself. Another wave of vomit pushes out of me, splattering the floor. Nice, Glenn. You pass out somewhere like a bum, and you then puke on the floor. Really nice.

I still have my coat on, and my dick is in my pants, so that's good news. I check for my phone. It's been missing for weeks, but I check out of habit anyway. I check my wallet and find it mercifully present. I'll worry about its contents later, but I can already tell it's lighter than the night before.

I appear to be in a utility closet of some kind, maybe in the back of the bar? I certainly spent enough money there last night, so maybe they tossed me in the back to sleep it off? Daylight outlines the shape of the door, so I can finally get out of the dark. I am not in the bar. In fact, I have no idea where I am. The beige walls, generic paintings of flowers every few feet, soft florescent lights; this could be anywhere. A hospital, maybe? Wouldn't be the first time. Maybe a rehab. But how did I get in the closet then? And where is everyone?

Pieces of last night start to roll in and I wince. It all got out of hand so quickly. It wasn't supposed to be a crazy night. I just wanted to get a drink or two. It was the first anniversary of my divorce, and I had just gotten my disability check. Just a drink or two and then back to the house. I had called Bill on the landline to bum a ride into town, but he answers my calls less and less these days. Another one bites the dust.

But I still wanted a drink, so I went alone. I walked down to McHebes, which is a real nasty pit of a bar. It sits just down the hill from my house, next to a 7-11 and across the street from the cheapest funeral home in town. I know that because they had done my mom's funeral, and I hate the fucking place.

My head throbs and a searing pain shoots through my ribs. I start to piece together last night-- I remember buying a drink, and then another, and then a few more. I remember mouthing off about something… and then I remember getting kicked out for trying to shove money down the bartender's tits. Used to be a time when women thought that kind of thing was funny, but I guess she didn't. She screamed like hell and the next thing I know, that bouncer prick is manhandling me and I've got a boot in my ass and a mouthful of pavement. People just can't take a joke anymore.

Lost in thought, I round the corner and realize where I am. I've come into a sterile room that I remember too well-- a table, some tattered chairs, a sample book of urns. I am in the funeral home.

I must have stumbled across the street, though I have no idea how I got inside. Did I break into this place? This is real, real bad. I'm on parole for another month and I'm not even supposed to be in a bar, let alone breaking and entering. I shake my head hard, trying to clear my thoughts. I gotta get the fuck outta here, fast, because there is no way that the cops are gonna laugh this one o--

"What are you doing here, Glenn?"

A woman who wasn't there before is sitting at the head of the table. She's wearing a cheap suit, and has a face like a rose long past bloom. She studies me over her glasses.

Fuck. This woman knows me. I'm suddenly very aware of the way I look. Besides being splattered with puke, when was the last time I showered? Washed these clothes? For the first time in a long time I'm self-conscious.

"H-How do you know-?"

"You don't remember me, Glenn?" the woman asks. A vague memory surfaces. This room, that chair-- this was the Funeral Director who had helped my sister, Joan, and I arrange my mom's funeral. What was her name? Was it Mindy? No, something with a B...

"Brenda," she answers for me. "I helped you and Joan arrange your mother's funeral"

"Yeah, yeah, sorry Brenda. That time was a blur for me."

"Yes, I imagine it was," she says blankly.

Another unbidden memory broke the surface. Mom's funeral last April. I'd started drinking when I woke up at eight, so by the time the service started at ten I was three sheets to the wind. There was an argument. My dickhead brother-in-law got in my face over something, probably the money Joan was giving me. He was always giving me shit about that. At my mother's fucking funeral, no less. I still don't know what my sister sees in that jar head prick.

It's a bit of a blur after that, but I woke up with stitches in my hand and a restraining order. That was the last time I saw Joan. And of course Brenda had been there; she had seen the whole thing.

"Glenn, why don't you sit down here for a second and talk to me. Have some water."

My good sense says no, but I'm so thirsty. My head feels like an angry beehive. I lower into the chair and take the frosty bottle she offers. The first sips of cold water are nirvana on my scorched throat.

"So, Glenn, why are you in the funeral home?" Brenda asks in a way that implies she already knows the answer. She lets the awkward silence hang before continuing.

"You look awful, Glenn. Betcha feel like shit too. I know what is going on with you and believe it or not, I can relate. I think I might be able to help you." Brenda reaches over to her purse and pulls out an AA chip: "Five Years Sober."

Oh no, fuck that. Water is one thing, but this? No fucking way. I need a nap and a joint, not this old bag lecturing me about rock bottom. Muttering excuses and apologies, I stand up to leave.

"Ok, go ahead. I'm not going to keep you here. But--" Brenda looks at me over the top of her glasses again, "If you were to leave, I am afraid I would need to notify the police that I found you here this morning. You don't want that, do you?"

Goddamn this bitch. She fixes me with flinty eyes. Shamed, I lower myself back into the chair.

"I don't hold it against you, I'm real familiar with the cops in this town. My daddy did a life sentence on an installment plan, and I spent a night or two in the drunk tank myself back in the day. Still, just talk to me for a few minutes, let me say my piece, and you can go. Okay?"

Seeing no way out of it, I resign. I vaguely remember my first trip here, to make plans for the funeral. Joan had sobbed miserably the whole time, worried about the strangest things. She had asked Brenda if our mom was going to need a coat because it would be cold in her casket underground. She was consumed with grief. Joan and Mom were so close. Joan was always over there towards the end. Making Mom food, cleaning. I should have helped her more. She was always good to me. I coulda been nicer to Joan, helped out, gone over to see Mom more. Then maybe Joan wouldn't have been so quick to side with her douchebag husband. A familiar wave of regret and self loathing wash over me.

"...knotted up, tight like a lock."

"Huh?" I had drifted off and didn't hear her.

"I said, when you drink the way you do it's because you're not dealing with something. You're using alcohol to lock that something out. But alcohol is a really shitty lock, and that thing behind the door is getting bigger and bigger, it is still seeping through until you have to drink more to deal with it. You need a key for that lock. You have to let it out and face it head on."

As she spoke Brenda stood up, walked to the window that over-looked the parking lot. The morning light was harsh on her weathered face. Her dyed black hair was scraped into a ponytail and a faded tattoo peaked over her shirt collar.

"I met my first husband, King, at a biker bar. He ran his own little gang, the Holy Cobras. First drinking, then snorting speed, staying up all night. That was the beginning of the end for me. Many long years of abuse, drinking, prison, more abuse. I was trapped."

My head is throbbing. I want coffee. I want her to stop talking. What does her bullshit life have to do with me? I think of lowering my shades, sitting in my easy boy chair. I attempt to make another break for it.

"Listen Brenda, I'm sorry but I'm really not feeling good so--"

"Where is Krystal, Glenn?"

The name hits me like a punch. I had forgotten that Brenda had met Krystal. She had come to my mom's funeral. We were on a "trial separation," but she had come anyway. Even wore her wedding ring. Brenda studied my expression before leaning forward to speak directly to my face like a child.

"Do you know why she left, Glenn?"

"I don't know, Brenda, why don't you tell me?" I snapped. "Since you're all dried out and you know every damn thing. Tell me why my wife left me."

"Because you're an asshole." Brenda grinned, totally unfazed by my outburst. "She left you because when you drink, you act like an asshole. At some point, that might have been the alcohol's fault. But now it's your fault, Glenn. You're an asshole."

Anger. Anger because she's right. Anger because she doesn't know the half of it. Anger because that's just not fucking fair. I had needed Krystal.

I needed her after I lost my job. I needed her after my mom died. I needed Krystal and she left me. What happened to "for better or for worse?" Why am I the villain?

Brenda lit a cigarette. The water bottle perspired on the table in front of me. It was still full. Brenda sighed smoke out of her nose before speaking.

"Yeah, my second husband left me because of my drinking too. That was my key moment. I couldn't stand to look at myself in the mirror anymore. We reconnected when I was sober but he had remarried. He was happier with his new wife. Getting sober doesn't fix everything, but it makes it easier to deal with."

I don't know if Krystal is happier without me or not. I remember the screaming matches, the 911 calls. But she was my wife, she was supposed to stand by me. Now I've lost them all. First Krystal, then my mom, and then Joan. But it all started when Krystal left. That was when the wheels just fell right the fuck off. Bills piled up, the house went to shit, and all I could do was pour myself another drink. To my horror, tears were streaming down my face. Brenda reached over to touch my hand, but thought better of it. She smoked instead.

"I know, Glenn," she said gently. "I know. It's okay."

Brenda's voice was kind. It had been so long since anyone was kind to me. Memories rush in all at once now; a memory of my mom when she wasn't sick, singing Motown in the kitchen. Joan and I as kids on Halloween, The Cowardly Lion and Dorothy. And Krystal, sweet Krystal. Krystal kissing me awake in the morning. Krystal humming "Sweet Caroline" while picking tomatoes in the garden, and how the sun shone through her hair. Then memories of Krystal helping me get to bed when I was too drunk. Krystal screaming at me for puking in the hallway again. Krystal crying as a police officer took me away in handcuffs.

Tears, hot and voluminous, run down my face. I am gasping, sobbing. Brenda is a blur, but her voice is clear.

"Glenn, what would you say to them? What would you say if they were here now?"

I think about it, the anger and the hurt. I think about the loss and the betrayal. But what I say comes out different. A part of me, pushed down by drink and numbed for years, slips out. "I-I would say I'm sorry. I shoulda stopped drinking. I would say that they deserved better. Krystal, Joan, my Mom--they all deserved better. I shoulda been better."

The release is immense. My face burns but I'm lighter than I've felt in years, than I've ever felt. I'm not even hungover anymore. Though my vision is fading I can see Brenda smiling at me.

"Alright Glenn, there's your key. I think you can go now."

---

Brenda set up the chapel for the service. She hummed "Sweet Caroline" as she lit candles and arranged the flowers. A surprising number of people had sent flowers, but the largest arrangement came from the bouncer at McHebes, Brandon. Glenn's family had decided to not press charges against Brandon for the fall that killed Glenn. They knew Glenn probably deserved it, and the coroner said if the skull fracture hadn't killed him, alcohol poisoning likely would have. The fact of the matter was that Glenn was not meant to make it home from the bar that night.

Brenda straightened the prayer cards, each featuring a picture of Glenn from better times. Before he became so angry, before he turned to drink. Brenda had not met this Glenn, but she found herself wishing she had. She checked her watch. Just a few minutes until the family is due to arrive. Snubbing out her cigarette, she lifted the casket lid.

Glenn looked pretty good for a guy who had bled out over a week ago, and a hell of a lot better than when Brenda saw him in the conference room that morning. Poor Glenn. He kept coming back, sick and confused, lost in his own personal purgatory. Most of the time people only come to talk to Brenda once, but it had taken Glenn a few tries. But this morning he found the key and let himself out. It was good timing, because after today he was off to his final resting place. Brenda had already written an anonymous letter to Joan to tell her that her brother had repented. That he had been himself at the very end, that he was sorry for how he had treated the people who loved him, that he wished he had stopped drinking.

People began to arrive, filing into the chapel. Brenda adjusted the velvet in the casket, and looked at Glenn one last time. Glenn's corpse looked peaceful, resting at last. She knew that his placid expression was more than just the success of a skilled embalmer. Glenn was finally at peace, and this hangover would truly be his last.

# THE SIREN

Brookings was a seaside town, a quaint hamlet perched on the beach above the Pacific Ocean. The majority of the town's income came from beach tourists in the summer months, when the ocean was deceptively kind. But they all cleared out in September. Not just the tourists; all the candy stores and burger shops boarded shut for the winter months too. That was when the ocean churned and raged, revealing its true nature. During winter Brookings was a ghost town, and that is why Anton went there for the week between Christmas and New Year's.

Not that he had anywhere else to go. His parents were long dead. His wife now lived in his former home with her boyfriend. Anton vaguely remembered going to Brookings on vacations as a child, and a solitary beach vacation at a bed and breakfast had seemed a pleasant alternative to yet another night alone in his dreary apartment.

But now that he was here, Anton was lonely and cold. He was trying to enjoy an evening walk on the beach, but the mist was so thick he could barely see before him. The roar of the ocean was not as comforting as he had remembered. It sounded like the churn of some great machine, crushing and destroying indiscriminately.

He was so focused on his walking that it took Anton a while to see the hulking mass in his path. At first he thought it was a boulder, one of the many that dotted the pebbled shore. But then the great creature began to move; it was massive, covered with moss and slimy seaweed. Its movements were crustacean-like, pulling the ground from under its body with rocky appendages and dragging along the shoreline. It was organic and ancient, something from the bottom of the sea.

In his horror Anton still thought the creature was strangely graceful. It raised its great craggy head, from which emerged twisted horns. As it dragged itself towards the furious sea the creature raised a rope net filled with something gently clattering. The rope bag was full of human skulls.

Anton let out a strangled gasp. The horned head turned, and Anton felt the gaze upon him. But the creature had no eyes, only hollow sockets. His stomach dropped. He was awash in the feeling that he did something wrong. The moment seemed endless. Anton blinked, and the creature was gone. In a flash it had leapt its great bulk into the sea. The surf rocked and rolled around it, and Anton watched as the tip of the monster's horns dipped beneath the sea foam.

He ran. The impossibility of it, what was that? Maybe it was man-made? Some kind of joke? But who would do that and why? He couldn't breathe-- the air felt too thick, it made him feel like he was drowning. At one point in his running the sand changed to tarmac, and he found himself

outside of the village store. An open sign glowed dimly, next to a note--
"YOUR VILLAGE SHOP, USE IT OR LOSE IT."

Anton went inside. A surly woman, wrapped in a wool coat and hat,
sat behind the counter. Anton felt disoriented. He couldn't find the words
to explain what had just happened to him.

"You gonna buy something? Or just stand there?" snapped
the woman.

"I saw... saw something on the beach..."

"What?"

"I saw... monster, with horns..."

Anton did not know what he hoped to accomplish by his confes-
sion. Maybe he thought that if he said it out loud it would be less real.
Maybe he hoped that this woman would have some kind of explanation.
But she didn't. Her ruddy face beneath her coat turned white. She stood up
abruptly and pointed to the door.

"Get out."

"What? I didn't m-"

"GET OUT! And STAY OUT!"

Anton stumbled out, bewildered. The woman slammed the door and
he heard the lock click as the open sign turned off. Again he was alone, and
the air was full of the churning sound of the ocean.

There was one other open shop on the street. The sign read "Pacific
Bookshop, Oddities and Antiquities." It was almost completely dark now,
and the shop's windows glowed warmly. Anton entered the tiny shop, its
shelves laden with dusty tomes, the walls cluttered with old maps and
ship blueprints.

"Can I help you?" An old man was behind the register. He was white haired and regarded Anton over half moon spectacles. His finger was paused over the page he had been interrupted reading.

Anton was calmer now. The warm shop soothed him. Not wanting to appear crazy to the shop owner, Anton didn't mention his run-in with the market woman or the creature he had just seen. Instead he panted, "Open during the holidays, huh?"

"Yep," said the old man, closing his book. "Me and the missus are full time down here. We live above the shop, so we just keep it open. Besides, the beach is more peaceful during the winter."

Anton's eyes ran over the cluttered shelves. Old knick knacks, seahorses in acrylic, and bronze ships. Then something horribly familiar caught his eye.

In a lighted glass case was a whale bone with an engraving of the creature Anton had seen on the beach. The horns, the rocky face; it was all illuminated--right down to the rope bag of skulls.

The shopkeeper followed Anton's stunned gaze to the glass case.

"Ah! My pride and joy. Are you familiar with scrimshaw? It is engravings on bone, usually a whale bone or walrus tusk. This one is a whale bone, eighteenth century. Created in this very town."

"W-what's on it?"

"A creature of local lore. The locals call it a siren, sinker of ships and drowner of man! Not like the beauties of the Odyssey, huh?"

Anton felt the icy glare of the creature on him again. No, this was not a fairytale beauty. This was a creature of death. Anton thought he tasted salt water in his mouth. He felt cold.

"Legend has it that those who see it are doomed to die at sea. Just another part of our rich folklore. And it makes sense with all the shipwrecks up here. Hundreds of people met their end on those rocks out there. You know they used to call this stretch of beach the "Graveyard of the Pacific?"

Anton couldn't look away from the scrimshaw figure. He backed up out of the shop, muttering apologies to the shop owner and bumping into side tables. The shop owner watched, curious and concerned, as Anton fled the shop and disappeared into the mist.

That night, Anton had bad dreams.

He dreamt he was back on the shores of the beach, cold wind whipping his face, staring into the turbulent water. All around him was the wreckage of ships. Their skeletons rose high above him, rotten and rusted. The wind beat against their crumpled flanks, howling through broken masts. And on the wind came another noise, a gentle sound in the crashing din, a song. A welcoming song. And inside the churning water he saw the creature. Felt the hollow cold stare of the eyes, and a song-- a beautiful song...

Anton wasn't on the beach. He was somewhere cold and dark. The ground below him listed wildly, and screaming people pressed against him on all sides. Though panicked, Anton thought about how this was the most he had been touched by another person in months. The ground rolled again, bringing with it more screams. In the darkness there was a deafening crunch of wood on stone. The screams-- cold water rushing all around him, lifting and twisting him. He had a few feet of air, he could just touch the rough wood ceiling. Above him thumping footsteps of sailors, cries for help. The flailing and thrashing of people all around him, hands grasping at his clothes. The water rose. He could touch the wood ceiling. Then his face was against it. The water filled his nose and mouth and lungs and he couldn't find any more air, just cold water.

He heard the song. The song of the creature filled his mind, encouraging him to let go. The other passengers bumped around him, their bodies now stiff and lifeless. They were now one with the shipwreck and the rocks and the sea. And Anton was among them. He had transformed from a single lonely man to a part of something larger. He was now part of a force of nature, folding into the moving currents and pressures as alive as blood in veins. His mind filled with the beautiful song of the siren and he allowed himself to be pulled away. He was no longer cold. He was no longer alone.

His eyes opened. Through the windows of his room at the Bed and Breakfast he heard the call of the ocean, the song of the siren.

---

The shopkeeper moved quietly around his kitchen. These last few years he had gotten up before dawn to have some coffee and watch the sunrise on the water. Though there wasn't much sunrise these months, the dark winter months. The sea gets real mean in the winter, and the shores are haunted with its victims. Some nights he thought he could hear them-- the wailing of doomed passengers, pulled down by the uncaring sea.

As he waited for the water to boil, the old man saw something out of the corner of his eye. It looked like a man, a man running into the wild surf. It was far off; the shopkeeper thought it looked like the man that had visited yesterday, the one who was so taken by the scrimshaw. But that could not be the case. No one would go swimming this time of year, in this surf. He turned away to pour coffee, and when he turned back the man was gone. The shopkeeper shook his head. It was surely a trick of the light.

No one would brave those waters-- unless they wanted to be buried in the graveyard of the Pacific.

# THE HOUSE ON LAUREL LANE

Have you ever heard of "being on someone's wavelength"? You seem to know what they're going to say before they say it? That could be familiarity, or a lucky guess. But not all the time. Sometimes it's something else. There are times when the pathway of feeling is permeable. Places can be like this too; a place can be so powerfully charged with feeling that it infiltrates others. Dark places can sense fear and pain. These places of pain reach out blindly, grasping, hunting for suffering similar to theirs. Suffering it can pull into itself. The Robertson Murder House was one such place.

Everyone in Hillside, New Jersey knew of the Robertson house. The story is still told at sleepovers, around campfires, and in locker rooms. The details often change. Some say that Mr. Roberston had eaten his victims for dinner, others say that he had sacrificed them to Satan. Either way Grant Robertson was the official boogeyman of Hillside, appearing in the nightmares of local children who dared each other to ring the doorbell of the house but never went inside.

The 1950s murders were such a part of the town's culture that there was briefly talk of turning the house itself, a nondescript colonial on Laurel Lane, into a museum dedicated to the grisly homicides. But the house remained abandoned. Besides, the older residents who lived in the town would be horrified. Their generation believed a community should hide such travesties.

It was this nexus of local legend that drew Alexis and Tamika out of their dorm rooms on a Sunday afternoon. Alexis guided her beater car along the increasingly rural highways while Tamika vibrated with excitement in the passenger seat, flipping through her binder of methodical notes.

"You know there are a lot of rumors that he ate them…"

"Uh-huh."

"But they are exactly that, *rumors*. Grant Robertson was not a cannibal and I feel that accusing him of that removes the weightiness of his crimes and—"

"Wait, he wasn't a cannibal? My best friend's sister said he was. Very reliable source." Alexis grinned at Tamika, who sniffed. Tamika wanted to be a librarian, and this paper on Grant Robertson was going to be her big thesis paper. Alexis didn't really care about this, but she liked Tamika. She also needed a break from campus, because the man Alexis had been dating for the past two months had just announced his engagement to another woman. On the outside she kept it together, but whenever she was alone she cried. So when Tamika said she needed to go on a trip, Alexis offered to drive.

Alexis glanced at the book of notes in Tamika's lap. Tamika had gone so far as to purchase back copies of local newspapers so she could have physical articles to reference. Tamika had her scrapbook open to one such article, featuring a large picture of Grant Robertson's face.

Grant Roberston had been a grim man with graying temples and horn-rimmed glasses. He didn't look like a monster, he looked like he worked at the DMV. Alexis supposed that's what had made the murders so terrifying; Grant Robertson had just been a "normal man" before he snapped and brutally murdered his whole family.

To another woman this might be an upsetting thought, but Alexis was no stranger to violence. She had been born into poverty. Her biological father had supported them by making and selling meth. Alexis didn't really remember him, he had shot and killed during a drug deal gone bad when Alexis was six years old. Her mother, sober and older now, had escaped poverty by re-marrying a dentist and erasing all traces of her past.

Alexis's stepdad wasn't exactly the paternal type either. He resented Alexis, often referring to her as his wife's "extra baggage." Alexis's mother then proceeded to have four more replacement kids, each one pushing Alexis further and further out of the family. When Alexis got a full ride scholarship to state college, she packed up her car and never looked back. The unwanted child shoved out of the family for good. To Alexis, the Robertson murders were just a highly magnified normal problem-- a father acting like a selfish dickhead.

What was shocking about the Laurel Lane case was that Grant Robertson never gave a satisfying motive for his family annihilation. Alexis and Tamika had watched his final recorded interview before the electric chair, and it was there that Grant admitted that he had killed his family because he was tired of them. That was all. He had been tired of being a father and a husband, so he bludgeoned his kin to death in their own home. During the interview Grant Robertson's face never changed-- grey, drawn, and blank.

Tamika continued to lecture Alexis on forensics and possible theories while the highways turned to roads, to streets, and finally they found the sleepy town of Hillside. They located the house right away, which is good because the locals weren't likely to give them directions. It was set far back from the road, wreathed in a lawn of scrub grass, the only visible part of the house being the mangy roof and the long chimney. It reminded Alexis of a tombstone. Nothing about that empty shell of a place indicated that it had ever been warm and inviting.

Tamika hopped out and made a beeline for the house. Alexis slammed her door and leaned against the hood of her car. She didn't want to admit it, but she was afraid to get closer to the house. What was there to see, anyway? The house was surrounded by a chain link fence, dotted with "no trespassing" signs.

Alexis stared at the front of the house and was just about to resume contemplating her breakup when a movement caught her eye. In the far corner of the abandoned house, a man was standing in the shattered glass window. Square shouldered and confrontational, Alexis felt his glare before she saw it, like a cold hand on the back of her neck. The dark shadow in the window was blurred yet she felt she could hear it. "Get. Away. From. My. House," hissed the words in the back of her skull. The figure slowly backed away from the window and disappeared.

Alexis took off running to find Tamika. Abandoned houses are one thing, but abandoned houses with squatters, no way. Anyone holed up there would not be happy to be disturbed by two shit-eating college students and Alexis was not about to be put in a shallow grave for Tamika's term paper. She whispered Tamika's name, running towards the back of the house. No response. It had only been a few minutes, but somehow Tamika had already disappeared. Did he find her first?

The fence in the back of the house had a rust hole you could drive a car through. The back door was wide open, sagging off of its hinges like a broken jaw. The late afternoon sun shone into the house, illuminating a decrepit hallway. With mounting dread, Alexis saw small, fresh footsteps in the dust, headed into the house. Alexis's mind raced. Maybe the squatter didn't know one of them was in the house. If she was quiet, she could grab Tamika and maybe get out of there without anyone noticing. God help them.

She briefly considered calling the cops but dismissed it. Alexis's time with her father had made her distrustful of police, and every moment she spent here was another moment that Tamika was alone in the house. She had no choice. She had to go in after her. Alexis walked up the groaning back steps and reluctantly followed Tamika's footsteps in the dust, cursing her with every minute. It was so typical of Tamika to do something like this, without a care in the world as if no one ever—

The air rushed, the ground dropped out below her feet. Music crashed down the decrepit hallway. A 1950's ballad; it sounded fuzzy like it was being played off a record player. Alexis was about to turn and run, but the door she had come in was gone.

This is what the house had wanted. She was trapped.

She was staring down a long, dark hallway. It looked like a mine shaft. Something was moving in the darkness at the end. Someone was walking towards her—slowly, but with building speed and purpose.

She ran. The hallway went on forever, lined with doors. Some of the doors would slam shut as she ran by them, but when she rattled the doorknob it was locked. And the footsteps approached ever closer. No matter how hard she ran, no matter how many doors she passed, the footsteps got closer. If only she could duck down a different hallway, try to find a different way out.

As if answering her thought, one of the doors in the hallway creaked open, revealing a sliver of dusty sunlight. Alexis pushed through and found herself in the foyer, with its grand staircase and high vaulted ceiling. A filthy chandelier hung over the room, and a wet animal smell filled the air. From all around music continued to croon.

This was the room in which Grant Robertson had neatly laid the bodies of his wife, teenage son, preteen daughter, and twin girls. He had bludgeoned them all to death with a claw hammer, with the exception of the six-year-old twin girls, whom he had decapitated. He left their headless bodies down with the others and had placed their heads to the top of the stairs, looking down on the gruesome scene. Up to his death Grant Robertson offered no explanation as to how or why he had cut his youngest daughter's heads off.

The floor in front of Alexis began to twist and writhe. Blood bubbled up from beneath the floorboards, oozing towards her. Alexis knew this couldn't be real, but a drop of blood leapt up onto her jeans and it was unmistakable-- hot, fetid, human blood. Alexis turned to run but again, the door she had entered through was now a wall. The only other door was across the room, across the rolling puddle of blood which was now boiling, filling the room with a metallic smell so strong it hung like a mist. The footsteps started again from the top of the stairs. They rang through the house.

Alexis leapt across the foyer, narrowly avoiding the pool of blood, and bashed through the door on the other side. She was now in the kitchen. The music was playing again, but softer now. The kitchen wasn't like the rest of the house, not damaged and decrepit. It was a neat and tidy American dream. Sunshine poured in through the spotless windows, illuminating a woman standing at the stove with her back to Alexis. She was humming quietly to herself, swaying slightly. Alexis couldn't see her face, but she had on an A-line dress, kitten heels, and her black hair was neatly styled. A housewife from a bygone era.

Alexis didn't care if this was a hallucination anymore. It felt real, the danger was real, and Alexis knew it. Whatever was doing this hated her. It had trapped her and now it wanted to kill her.

The woman at the stove didn't acknowledge Alexis, didn't even seem to know she was there. Alexis was about to search for an exit but the footsteps approached again, sudden. Loud. The woman ceased her swaying and cocked her head to one side, listening. "Grant? Honey is that yo—"

Then there was a deafening BANG. The back of the woman's head slumped, blood splattering on the floor and ceiling. BANG. The other side of the woman's head caved in, and she fell to the floor heavily. BANG BANG BANG. An invisible force battered the woman's head into a pulp and slung blood in arcs against the ceiling. The woman's body twitched convulsively, her hands fluttering against the floor like startled birds. The blows stopped, and again Alexis felt the glare, the cold hand on the back of her neck. And the footsteps came for her.

She backed away. The room elongated. The music slowed to an eerie, low dirge. Blood darkened the floor around the woman's now motionless body. The footsteps felt as if they were right in front of Alexis. She felt the resentment and rage with each approaching step as sure as vibrations in the floorboards.

"Alexis. Come here."

Tamika's voice whispered into her ear. Alexis jumped, and the walls began to melt away.

Now she was in a bedroom. The walls were papered with sports posters and the room was neat and bright like the kitchen had been. It smelled of clean laundry and dirt, as well as the unmistakable musky aroma of a teenage boy's room. But under it there was another smell, the filth of the rotting house.

In the shadowed corner of the room stood Tamika. Alexis couldn't see her face, but her silhouette looked like she was shaking with mirth, as if this was some sort of hilarious joke that only she was in on.

"Tamika this isn't f-funny, stop f-fucking around—" Alexis stammered, taking a step towards the darkened figure. The shape continued to twitch and writhe in shadow.

It wasn't Tamika.

A mostly headless teenage boy lurched out of the corner. What was left of his face slumped in a mass of teeth and hair. Blood and lymphatic fluid dripped down the front of his letterman's jacket. He ran at Alexis, reaching for her piteously. Her nerve finally broke and she screamed.

She was back in the long, wallpapered hallway. The boy was gone, and she felt a rush of relief. But something was wrong with the perspective. The hallway seemed to be breathing gently, elongating and shortening. She couldn't hear the footsteps but Alexis knew they were there with her. He was silhouetted at the end of the hallway. He was faceless and covered in blood. He was holding a claw hammer, and he was coming for her.

"No! Dad, NO!" Alexis blurted out. But this man wasn't her father. her father had been dead sixteen years. But it was, she knew it was her father.

The figure walked down the hallway towards her, not running, but marching with a purpose. Alexis pushed herself backwards. She was back in the foyer again and she tripped over the body of little Nellie Robertson, Grant Robertson's middle child. Nellie had fought back against her father and died the slowest death of them all. The twins' crumpled bodies were in a heap at the bottom of the stairs like discarded trash, blood soaking their matching dresses.

Thunk. Thunk. Thunk. Down the stairs rolled the head of Jamie Robertson, followed by her sister Millie, as she had been in life. The heads rolled to Alexis's feet and they stared up at her with expressions of biblical anguish, eyes rolled back into their skulls, white blonde hair matted with blood and filth, mouths open in screams that were never to come.

Slowly descending after the severed heads was the father, ready to finish his task. Grant Robertson was upon Alexis, raising his hammer, ready to deliver his justice. Then it wasn't Grant Robertson, it was Alexis's own stepfather, ready to get rid of Alexis once and for all. And then it was her dead father, face ruined from the shotgun blast, stumbling towards her with the hammer raised. Grant Robertson. Her stepfather. Her father. All swirling into one darkened shadow, raising the hammer high to bring it down on her unwanted, burdensome head.

Alexis wailed, she clutched her face. She didn't want this, she hadn't asked to be here, she hadn't asked to be born to a world that didn't want her, to hammers and violence and men who only saw one way out. She hadn't asked for any of this.

"ALEXIS! Alexis! Jesus Christ stop screaming!"

Tamika was standing in front of her clasping her arms to her sides, shaking her, dark eyes wide with concern behind her glasses. It was darker now. They were outside the fence. There was no hole, the door to the house was double locked. Alexis stared down at her hands and saw that they were filthy.

"What hap—"

"You tell me!" Tamika screamed, angry and terrified. "I just went around the back of the house to take some pictures and you fucking disappeared! I've been looking for you for an hour! I just found you here a minute ago, clinging to the fence and screaming! For Christ's sake what is wrong with you?"

Alexis began sobbing softly, still staring at her dirt covered hands and knees. In the twilight her tear streaked face made her look like a hurt child. Tamika, now a different kind of panicked, put a hand on her shoulder.

"Are you okay? Did you see someone else? Did they hurt you?" Tamika offered, alarmed at this expression. She had never seen Alexis cry.

"Yeah," Alexis whispered, "yeah, but they're gone now." In her mind she could still see the hammer raising, still hear the footsteps coming for her, always coming for her. She limply handed Tamika her car keys, and Tamika hustled them back to the car. Their tires squealed as they rushed from the house. The night darkened. The husk of a house retreated, sinking into the grass and trees, as if it had never been there at all.